King Arthur and his Knights

亞瑟王和他的圓桌武士

U0106939

商務印書館

出版説明

　　本館一向倡導優質閱讀，近年來連續推出了以"Q"為標識的 "Quality English Learning 優質英語學習"系列，其中《讀名著學英語》叢書，更是香港書展入選好書，讀者反響令人鼓舞。推動社會閱讀風氣，推動英語經典閱讀，藉閱讀拓廣世界視野，提高英語水平，已經成為一種潮流。

　　然良好閱讀習慣的養成非一日之功，大多數初、中級程度的讀者，常視直接閱讀厚重的原著為畏途。如何給年輕的讀者提供切實的指引和幫助，如何既提供優質的學習素材，又提供名師的教學方法，是當下社會關注的重要問題。針對這種情況，本館特別延請香港名校名師，根據多年豐富的教學經驗，精選海外適合初、中級英語程度讀者的優質經典讀物，有系統地出版了這套叢書，名為《Black Cat 優質英語階梯閱讀》。

　　《Black Cat 優質英語階梯閱讀》體現了香港名校名師堅持經典學習的教學理念，以及多年行之有效的學習方法。既有經過改寫和縮寫的經典名著，又有富創意的現代作品；既有精心設計的聽、說、讀、寫綜合練習，又有豐富的歷史文化知識；既有彩色插圖、繪圖和照片，又有英美專業演員朗讀作品的 CD。適合口味不同的讀者享受閱讀之樂，欣賞經典之美。

　　《Black Cat 優質英語階梯閱讀》由淺入深，逐階提升，好像參與一個尋寶遊戲，入門並不難，但要真正尋得寶藏，需要投入，更需要堅持。只有置身其中的人，才能體味純正英語的魅力，領略得到真寶的快樂。當英語閱讀成為自己生活的一部分，英語水平的提高自然水到渠成。

商務印書館（香港）有限公司
編輯部

使用說明

◆ **應該怎樣選書？**

按閱讀興趣選書

《Black Cat 優質英語階梯閱讀》精選世界經典作品，也包括富於創意的現代作品；既有膾炙人口的小說、戲劇，又有非小說類的文化知識讀物，品種豐富，內容多樣，適合口味不同的讀者挑選自己感興趣的書，享受閱讀的樂趣。

按英語程度選書

《Black Cat 優質英語階梯閱讀》現設 Level 1 至 Level 6，由淺入深，涵蓋初、中級英語程度。讀物分級採用了國際上通用的劃分標準，主要以詞彙（vocabulary）和結構（structures）劃分。

Level 1 至 Level 3 出現的詞彙較淺顯，相對深的核心詞彙均配上中文解釋，節省讀者查找詞典的時間，以專心理解正文內容。在註釋的幫助下，讀者若能流暢地閱讀正文內容，就不用擔心這一本書程度過深。

Level 1 至 Level 3 出現的動詞時態形式和句子結構比較簡單。動詞時態形式以現在時（present simple）、現在時進行式（present continuous）、過去時（past simple）為主，句子結構大部分是簡單句（simple sentences）。此外，還包括比較級和最高級（comparative and superlative forms）、可數和不可數名詞（countable and uncountable nouns）以及冠詞（articles）等語法知識點。

Level 4 至 Level 6 出現的動詞時態形式，以現在完成時（present perfect）、現在完成時進行式（present perfect continuous）、過去完成時（past perfect continuous）為主，句子結構大部分是複合句（compound sentences）、條件從句（1st and 2nd conditional sentences）等。此外，還包括情態動詞（modal verbs）、被動形式（passive forms）、動名詞（gerunds）、

短語動詞（phrasal verbs）等語法知識點。

　　根據上述的語法範圍，讀者可按自己實際的英語水平，如詞彙量、語法知識、理解能力、閱讀能力等自主選擇，不再受制於學校年級劃分或學歷高低的約束，完全根據個人需要選擇合適的讀物。

② 怎樣提高閱讀效果？

　　閱讀的方法主要有兩種：一是泛讀，二是精讀。兩者各有功能，適當地結合使用，相輔相成，有事半功倍之效。

　　泛讀，指閱讀大量適合自己程度（可稍淺，但不能過深）、不同內容、風格、體裁的讀物，但求明白內容大意，不用花費太多時間鑽研細節，主要作用是多接觸英語，減輕對它的生疏感，鞏固以前所學過的英語，讓腦子在潛意識中吸收詞彙用法、語法結構等。

　　精讀，指小心認真地閱讀內容精彩、組織有條理、遣詞造句又正確的作品，着重點在於理解 "準確" 及 "深入"，欣賞其精彩獨到之處。精讀時，可充分利用書中精心設計的練習，學習掌握有用的英語詞彙和語法知識。精讀後，可再花十分鐘朗讀其中一小段有趣的文字，邊唸邊細心領會文字的結構和意思。

　　《Black Cat 優質英語階梯閱讀》中的作品均值得精讀，如時間有限，不妨嘗試每兩個星期泛讀一本，輔以每星期挑選書中一章精彩的文字精讀。要學好英語，持之以恆地泛讀和精讀英文是最有效的方法。

③ 本系列的練習與測試有何功能？

　　《Black Cat 優質英語階梯閱讀》特別注重練習的設計，為讀者考慮周到，切合實用需求，學習功能強。每章後均配有訓練聽、説、讀、寫四項技能的練習，分量、難度恰到好處。

聽力練習分兩類，一是重聽故事回答問題，二是聆聽主角對話、書信朗讀、或模擬記者訪問後寫出答案，旨在以生活化的練習形式逐步提高聽力。每本書均配有 CD 提供作品朗讀，朗讀者都是專業演員，英國作品由英國演員錄音，美國作品由美國演員錄音，務求增加聆聽的真實感和感染力。多聆聽英式和美式英語兩種發音，可讓讀者熟悉二者的差異，逐漸培養分辨英美發音的能力，提高聆聽理解的準確度。此外，模仿錄音朗讀故事或模仿主人翁在戲劇中的對白，都是訓練口語能力的好方法。

閱讀理解練習形式多樣化，有縱橫字謎、配對、填空、字句重組等等，注重訓練讀者的理解、推敲和聯想等多種閱讀技能。

寫作練習尤具新意，教讀者使用網式圖示（spidergrams）記錄重點，採用問答、書信、電報、記者採訪等多樣化形式，鼓勵讀者動手寫作。

書後更設有升級測試（Exit Test）及答案，供讀者檢查學習效果。充分利用書中的練習和測試，可全面提升聽、說、讀、寫四項技能。

❹ 本系列還能提供甚麼幫助？

《Black Cat 優質英語階梯閱讀》提倡豐富多元的現代閱讀，巧用書中提供的資訊，有助於提升英語理解力，擴闊視野。

每本書都設有專章介紹相關的歷史文化知識，經典名著更有作者生平、社會背景等資訊。書內富有表現力的彩色插圖、繪圖和照片，使閱讀充滿趣味，部分加上如何解讀古典名畫的指導，增長見識。有的書還提供一些與主題相關的網址，比如關於不同國家的節慶源流的網址，讓讀者多利用網上資源增進知識。

Contents

The story is recorded in full. 故事錄音

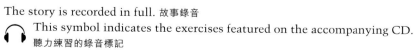 This symbol indicates the exercises featured on the accompanying CD.
聽力練習的錄音標記

Was King Arthur only a Legend?

No, King Arthur was not only a legend. In the ninth century, a historian called Nennius wrote a book called *Historia Britonum*. It was a history of Britain, about the life of the Celtic leader, Arthur, and his knights [1].

Nennius wrote that Arthur was a great Celtic military leader of the 5th and 6th century. He fought against the Saxons, from the year 513 to 537. He and his men won many battles against the Saxons.

His people loved and remembered him for centuries after. There are lots of old ballads [2], songs, poems and stories about Arthur and his knights.

In 1470, Sir Thomas Malory wrote about King Arthur and his castle, Camelot. His writings are a complete and accurate [3] record [4] of the King's life and times.

Today there are many books and films in different languages on this exciting subject [5]. King Arthur is so famous that he is part of the Briten literary cycle [6].

1. **knights**：武士。
2. **ballads**：民歌。
3. **accurate**：精確的。
4. **record**：記錄。
5. **subject**：主題。
6. **cycle**：循環。

Important Places During Arthur's Time

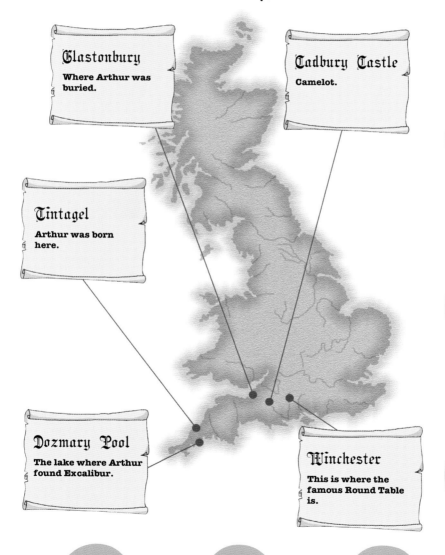

Glastonbury

Where Arthur was buried.

Cadbury Castle

Camelot.

Tintagel

Arthur was born here.

Dozmary Pool

The lake where Arthur found Excalibur.

Winchester

This is where the famous Round Table is.

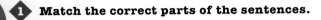

1 **Match the correct parts of the sentences.**

a. Nennius was

b. Nennius wrote that King Arthur

c. From the year 513 to 537

d. His people remembered him

e. Historia Britonum

1. with songs, poems and stories.

2. is a historic book about King Arthur and his times.

3. was a great Celtic leader of the 6th century.

4. Arthur fought against the Saxons.

5. a historian of the 9th century.

This is a medieval map of Britain in the year 600 A.D.

Before Arthur's Time

The first inhabitants [1] of Britain were probably the Celts. They came from Germany in the third century BC.

The Roman general [2], Julius Caesar, invaded [3] Britain in the year 54 BC. He had 25,000 soldiers and 2,000 horses. But he did not stay in Britain. He went to fight the Gauls in France.

In 43 AD. the Roman Emperor Claudius invaded Britain. This time the Romans stayed. Britain became a Roman province [4], called Britannia.

The Romans built roads, walls and towns. There are many Roman remains [5] in Britain. Hadrian's Wall is a good example. It was built by the Roman Emperor Hadrian in 122 AD. He built it in the north of Britain to keep out [6] the Scots. It is about 120 kilometres long. It took six years to build.

The Romans left Britain in 410 AD. after 350 years.

During the fifth and sixth century, the Angles and the Saxons invaded Britain. The legendary [7] King Arthur fought against these invaders and others.

These are two sides of a Roman coin. It was made to celebrate Claudius's victory in Britain. One side shows Emperor Claudius and the other shows him riding his horse. Notice the writing 'De Britann' on the coin.

1. **inhabitants** : 居民。
2. **general** : 將軍。
3. **invaded** : 侵略。
4. **province** : 省份。
5. **remains** : 遺跡。
6. **keep out** : 阻擋。
7. **legendary** : 傳奇性的。

1 Can you find the names of three Roman Emperors and the name of the Roman province? Circle them.

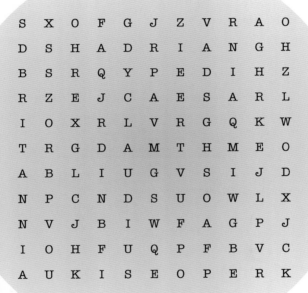

```
S  X  O  F  G  J  Z  V  R  A  O
D  S  H  A  D  R  I  A  N  G  H
B  S  R  Q  Y  P  E  D  I  H  Z
R  Z  E  J  C  A  E  S  A  R  L
I  O  X  R  L  V  R  G  Q  K  W
T  R  G  D  A  M  T  H  M  E  O
A  B  L  I  U  G  V  S  I  J  D
N  P  C  N  D  S  U  O  W  L  X
N  V  J  B  I  W  F  A  G  P  J
I  O  H  F  U  Q  P  F  B  V  C
A  U  K  I  S  E  O  P  E  R  K
```

BEFORE READING

What is a legend?

A legend begins as a true story, but as the years pass some things are added to it, and some things are forgotten.

So, a legend is a mix of historical facts and popular fantasy.

1 **What words do you think of when you hear these words: *King Arthur and his Knights*? Circle the words.**

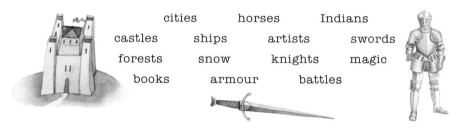

cities   horses   Indians

castles   ships   artists   swords

forests   snow   knights   magic

books   armour   battles

2 **What is your favourite legend?**

CHAPTER ONE

Young Arthur

In the year 493, Uther Pendragon became King of Britain. He had a counsellor [1] named Merlin. Merlin was also a magician [2].

When King Uther's son Arthur was born, Merlin said, 'Your son must grow up away from the court. It is safer!'

Merlin gave the baby son to Sir Ector and his wife. They raised [3] him well.

When King Uther died in 509, Britain had no king. The country had many problems.

Merlin went to the Archbishop of Canterbury [4] and said, 'Britain must have a king. We must find one. Call all the noblemen of the kingdom. Tell them to meet at the great church in London on

1. **counsellor**：顧問。
2. **magician**：巫師。
3. **raised**：撫養。
4. **Archbishop of Canterbury**：坎特伯雷主教。

Christmas Day. There, God will show us the new king.'

On Christmas Day, all the noblemen were in the great church. Outside the church there was a big stone with a sword in it. These words were written on the big stone:

He who pulls the sword out of this stone is the true King of Britain.

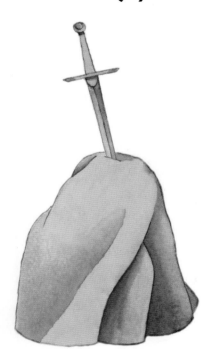

UNDERSTANDING THE TEXT

1 **Choose the correct answer.**

a. In the year 493
- [ ] Merlin was born
- [ ] Uther Pendragon became King of Britain
- [ ] King Arthur was born

b. Merlin, the magician, was
- [ ] King Uther's counsellor
- [ ] King Uther's father
- [ ] the Archbishop of Canterbury

c. Merlin gave King Uther's baby son to
- [ ] the church
- [ ] the Archbishop of Canterbury
- [ ] Sir Ector and his wife

d. In the year 509
- [ ] Merlin became the King's counsellor
- [ ] King Uther died
- [ ] Arthur was born

e. Merlin told the Archbishop of Canterbury
- [ ] 'God will show us the new king on Christmas Day'
- [ ] 'A nobleman of London is the new king'
- [ ] 'You must be the new king'

f. What was written on the stone?
- [ ] 'He who breaks this sword is the true King of Britain'
- [ ] 'He who pulls the sword out of this stone is the true King of Britain'
- [ ] 'He who pulls the sword out of this stone is the new Archbishop of Canterbury'

The Past Simple（過去時）

The Past Simple of a verb is often used to tell a story. Put the correct verb next to the Past Simple form. The anagram（變形詞）**of the infinitive**（動詞原形）**is in the stone.**

PAST	INFINITIVE
became	
had	
was	
died	
gave	
raised	
went	
said	

eb   vgei

ied   esria

ysa   og

mebeco   vhea

CHAPTER TWO

The Sword in the Stone

ach nobleman tried to pull the sword out of the stone. No one was able to do it.

On New Year's Day, the sword was still in the stone. Arthur was there with Sir Ector.

Arthur pulled the sword out of the stone without difficulty! This was the sign [1] from God. All the noblemen were surprised. He was the new King of Britain.

Sir Ector said, 'Arthur, you are now the King of Britain.'

Arthur said, 'Father, I don't want to leave you!'

1. **sign** : 示意。

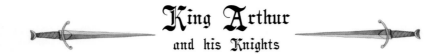

Sir Ector said, 'I'm not your real father. I don't know who you are. The magician Merlin brought you to us when you were born. I raised you like a son, and I love you. Now you are a king. God wants you to lead [1] Britain. You must go and do your duty [2].'

Merlin said to the noblemen, 'This is King Uther's son and he is our new king!'

Young Arthur first became a knight. Then he became King of Britain.

1. **lead**：統治。
2. **do your duty**：履行職責。

UNDERSTANDING THE TEXT

1 Decide whether these sentences are true (T) or false (F).

	T	F
a. No nobleman was able to pull the sword out of the stone.	☐	☐
b. Arthur was in London with Merlin.	☐	☐
c. Arthur pulled the sword out of the stone easily.	☐	☐
d. All the noblemen were angry.	☐	☐
e. Arthur became the new King of Britain.	☐	☐
f. Sir Ector was not Arthur's real father.	☐	☐
g. Merlin said, 'This is Sir Ector's son and he is our new king!'	☐	☐

2 Match the words below with their opposites.

a. first	**1.** come
b. pull	**2.** old
c. difficult	**3.** small
d. true	**4.** take
e. new	**5.** hate
f. born	**6.** push
g. big	**7.** false
h. bring	**8.** easy
i. love	**9.** die
j. go	**10.** last

3 Demonstrative Pronouns （指示代詞）

In Chapter 2, we saw this sentence:

This was the sign from God.

The Demonstrative Pronouns are: this, that, these **and** those.
This **and** these **refer to things close to you.** That **and** those **refer to things farther away.**

Complete the sentences below with a suitable demonstrative pronoun.

a. Today is Christmas Day, and all the noblemen are in the church. .... is an important day.

b. 'Who is the old man at the back of the church?' asked Arthur. '............... is the Archbishop of Canterbury,' said Sir Ector.

c. 'Look at the young boy here with the sword,' said Merlin. '............... is the new King of Britain.

d. Many men are in front of the church over there. .... are the noblemen of Britain.

e. .... are the words written on the stone in front of the church.

f. Sir Ector was outside the church. '............... is the great church of London,' he said.

 4 Listen to Chapter 2 and circle the words that you hear.

horse	sword	stone	forest
boat	King	Britain	mother
home		father	castle
clock	cold		
winter		magician	
		knight	

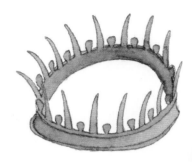

CHAPTER THREE

Britain has a King

rthur was a young king. He was about twenty years old. He lived at Camelot. His first years as king were difficult. He fought against many enemies from other lands, particularly the Saxons. Some noblemen of his court caused trouble [1]. They did not want to obey a young king.

King Arthur was very adventurous [2]. He liked riding his horse and looking for adventures. He was courageous, loyal [3] and friendly. His people loved him.

One day, King Arthur was riding in the forest. He saw a fountain [4]. Near the fountain there was a knight named Sir Pellinore.

'Stop!' said Sir Pellinore. 'You cannot go past the fountain! You must fight with me first!'

---

1. **trouble** : 麻煩。
2. **adventurous** : 愛冒險的。
3. **loyal** : 忠誠的。
4. **fountain** : 噴泉。

King Arthur
and his Knights

King Arthur answered, 'I'm ready to fight!' The two knights began fighting. First they fought with their lances [1]. Then they fought with their swords.

During the fight, Arthur's sword broke. Sir Pellinore said, 'I'm the winner!'

At that moment, Merlin appeared and said, 'Pellinore, this knight is your king! King Arthur!' Sir Pellinore stopped fighting immediately.

1. **lances :**

UNDERSTANDING THE TEXT

1 Fill in the blank spaces with the words from the sword.

courageous   Saxons   lances   adventures
swords   twenty   king   friendly   enemies   broke
Merlin   Pellinore

a. King Arthur was about .... years old.

b. He fought against the .... and other ....

c. He liked ....

d. His people loved him because he was .... and
....

e. King Arthur fought against Sir ....

f. The two knights fought with their .... and
....

g. During the fight, Arthur .... his sword.

h. Pellinore stopped fighting when .... said, 'This
knight is your ....!'

A. **Find the four hidden words that describe King Arthur. Circle them.**

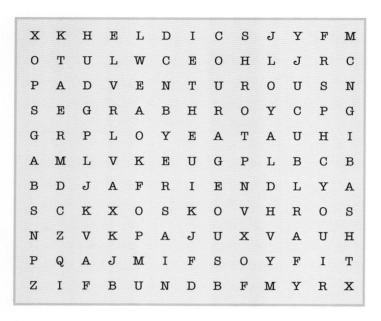

X	K	H	E	L	D	I	C	S	J	Y	F	M
O	T	U	L	W	C	E	O	H	L	J	R	C
P	A	D	V	E	N	T	U	R	O	U	S	N
S	E	G	R	A	B	H	R	O	Y	C	P	G
G	R	P	L	O	Y	E	A	T	A	U	H	I
A	M	L	V	K	E	U	G	P	L	B	C	B
B	D	J	A	F	R	I	E	N	D	L	Y	A
S	C	K	X	O	S	K	O	V	H	R	O	S
N	Z	V	K	P	A	J	U	X	V	A	U	H
P	Q	A	J	M	I	F	S	O	Y	F	I	T
Z	I	F	B	U	N	D	B	F	M	Y	R	X

B. **Now match the four hidden words with their meanings.**

A person who......

a. makes many friends is: ....

b. is not afraid is: ....

c. you can trust is: ....

d. likes doing exciting things is: ....

3 **Like + -ing**

The verb 'like' **is followed by the gerund** (動名詞) **. Look at this sentence:** 'He *liked* rid*ing* his horse and look*ing* for adventures.'
Fill in the gaps with the correct verbs from the box.

> **liked fighting   didn't like riding**
> **liked causing trouble   didn't like living   likes reading**
> **doesn't like eating**

a. He is never hungry. He ....

b. Sir Pellinore and Arthur fought with their swords. They
....

c. The noblemen did not obey Arthur. They ....

d. The Archbishop was afraid of horses. He ....

e. She read a book about King Arthur. She ....

f. The first Roman invaders did not stay in Britain. They
.... there.

4 **Arthur writes a letter to Sir Ector, telling him about the fight with Sir Pellinore. Put the verbs in the Past Simple tense** (過去時) **and add the articles** (冠詞) **, if necessary.**

Dear Father,
Yesterday / I / go / forest.
I / ride / my / beautiful horse.
In / forest / I / see / fountain.
My horse / want / to drink / some water.
I / meet / Sir Pellinore. He / say / 'Fight!'
I / fight / him but I / break / my sword!
Merlin / appear / and say: 'Stop fighting!'
Sir Pellinore / stop / fighting immediately.
Love, Arthur

Knights

The Knight was an important figure [1] in the feudal system [2] of the Middle Ages [3]. A knight was a warrior [4]. He defended his king, his country and his church. He was a strong, courageous figure. He protected women, children, the poor and the weak. He fought for justice. He was generous with everyone. This was the Code of Chivalry [5], which he obeyed. Knights usually came from rich and noble families. They started their training when they were very young, as pages. Then they became squires and finally knights. It was a great honour to become a knight. Knights formed a separate social class [6] in their kingdom.

Knights wore fine clothes. Their armour [7] was heavy. Even their horses wore heavy armour. When a knight fought, he usually carried a shield [8], a lance, a long sword, a battle-axe [9] and a knife. Each knight had a shield with a particular colour and design on it.

1. **figure**：人物。
2. **the feudal system**：封建體制。
3. **the Middle Ages**：(歐洲歷史上的) 中世紀。
4. **warrior**：武士。
5. **the Code of Chivalry**：武士行為準則。
6. **separate social class**：獨立的社會階層。

7. **armour**：
8. **shield**：
9. **battle-axe**：

Page
受訓武士

Age: from age 7 to the teen years
Duties: He learned to:
- serve and obey his superiors [1]
- ride a horse
- use weapons
- play special games
- hunt with falcons and hawks [2]

Squire
扈從

Age: from the teen years to 21 years old
Duties: He learned to:
- fight in battle
- serve his lord
- assist [3] his knight during a battle
- play Quintain, a battle sport

Knight
武士

Age: 21 years old
During an important ceremony [4], the squire was dressed in red and black. Here he received knighthood [5]. He promised to obey the Code of Chivalry. Now he was a knight and he served his king, queen or lord.

---

1. **superiors**：上級。
2. **falcons and hawks**：獵鷹。
3. **assist**：援助。
4. **ceremony**：儀式。
5. **knighthood**：武士身分。

The knight's armour and weapons

1 Complete the boxes.

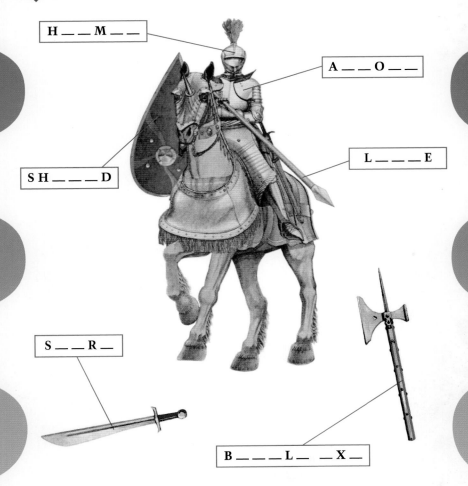

H _ _ M _ _

A _ _ O _ _

S H _ _ _ D

L _ _ _ E

S _ _ R _

B _ _ _ L _ _ X _

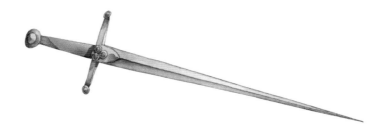

CHAPTER FOUR

Excalibur

rthur rode away with Merlin and said, 'I broke my sword during the fight with Sir Pellinore. I am king because of that sword. I must have another sword.'

'Come with me then,' said Merlin.

Arthur followed Merlin to a lake of clear water. In the middle of the lake, Arthur saw an arm. The arm was holding a sword in a beautiful scabbard [1].

'Look!' said Merlin. 'That is the sword and that is the Lady of the Lake. Ask her kindly and the sword is yours.'

Arthur saw a beautiful lady in a boat on the lake. He asked her, 'Can I have that sword?'

She answered, 'Yes, you can have it. Take my boat and go and get it.'

---

1. **scabbard** : 劍鞘。

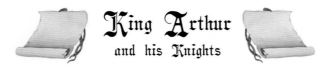

King Arthur
and his Knights

Arthur and Merlin went to the middle of the lake. There Arthur took the sword. He was very interested in it. He took the sword out of the scabbard and looked at it. It was a beautiful sword with jewels on it.

'Look, Merlin,' he said, 'the word Excalibur is written on it.'

'Yes, Excalibur is the greatest sword in the world. But its scabbard is more precious.'

'Why?' asked Arthur.

'It has a great magic power,' said Merlin. 'When you wear it, you never bleed [1] even if you are wounded [2]. When you fight, you must always have the scabbard with you.'

1. **bleed** : 流血。
2. **wounded** : 受傷。

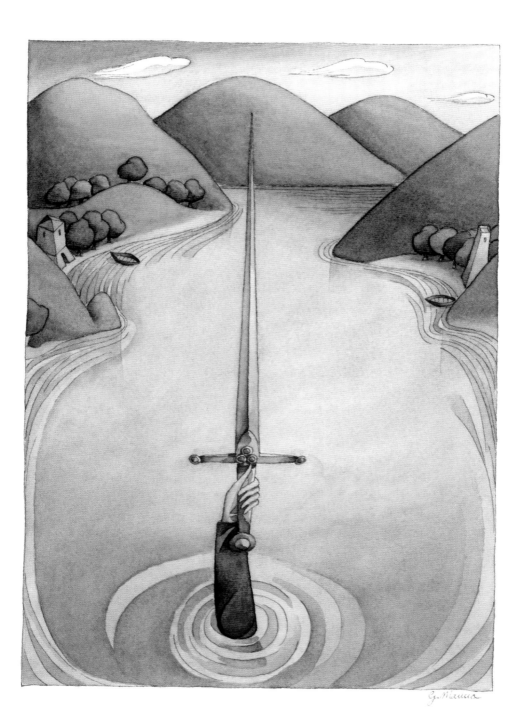

UNDERSTANDING THE TEXT

1 **Circle the correct answers.**

a. Arthur *lost / broke* his sword during the fight with Sir Pellinore. He told *Sir Pellinore / Merlin* about it.

b. Arthur followed Merlin to a *lake / forest*. In the middle of the *forest / lake*, there was *a stone / an arm*. It was holding a sword.

c. Arthur asked *Merlin / the Lady of the Lake*, 'Can I have the sword?'

d. Arthur and Merlin went to the middle of the lake. They *looked at / took* the sword.

e. Merlin said, 'Excalibur is the *biggest / greatest* sword in the world. Its scabbard has a *magic / hidden* power.'

f. 'When you *use / wear* it, you never *lose a battle / bleed*.'

2 **Prepositions** (介詞)

Fill in the blank spaces with the correct prepositions in the crown. Some words can be used twice.

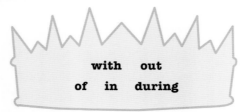

with   out

of   in   during

a. Arthur rode away .... Merlin.

b. Arthur broke his sword .... the fight with Sir Pellinore.

c. In the middle .... the lake, Arthur saw an arm holding a sword .... a beautiful scabbard.

d. He took the sword .... of the scabbard.

e. When you fight, you must always keep the scabbard .... you.

CHAPTER FIVE

Arthur meets Guinevere

 lot of enemies tried to invade Britain: the Saxons, the Jutes, the Pitts and others.

A big army of Saxons attacked King Leodegrance in his castle. He was the King of Cameliard. Young King Arthur and his knights fought against these Saxons and won.

King Leodegrance was very thankful [1] to Arthur. He invited him and his knights to a royal banquet [2]. At the banquet, Arthur met the King's daughter, Princess Guinevere. Guinevere was young and very beautiful. Arthur fell in love with her. He wanted to marry her.

1. **thankful** : 感激的。
2. **a royal banquet** : 王室宴會。

37

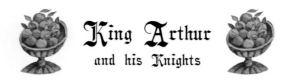

King Arthur
and his Knights

Merlin wasn't happy with Arthur's choice [1], but he accepted his king's decision.

King Leodegrance, Guinevere's father, was very happy about this marriage. 'I am honoured [2] to give my daughter to our courageous king!' said Guinevere's father. 'My gift to King Arthur is the Round Table, which belonged to his father, King Uther.'

Arthur and Guinevere were married. There was an enormous [3] banquet. Everyone in the kingdom was happy.

Guinevere arrived at King Arthur's castle with her ladies and the Round Table. The enormous Round Table had places for 150 knights. Arthur called the best knights of Britain to sit at the Round Table. Only the bravest knights were part of Arthur's court.

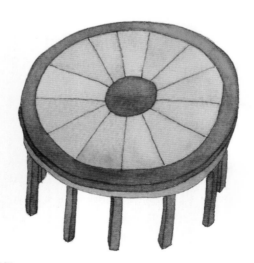

1. **choice**：選擇。
2. **honoured**：榮幸的。
3. **enormous**：巨大的。

UNDERSTANDING THE TEXT

1 **Choose the correct answer.**

a. The Saxons, Jutes and Pitts were
- [ ] tribes of southern Britain
- [ ] enemies of Britain
- [ ] friends of King Arthur

b. A big army of Saxons attacked
- [ ] King Arthur
- [ ] Camelot
- [ ] King Leodegrance's castle

c. King Arthur fought against the Saxons
- [ ] and won the battle
- [ ] and lost the battle
- [ ] and was wounded

d. King Leodegrance invited Arthur to a banquet
- [ ] but Arthur did not go
- [ ] and he met Princess Guinevere
- [ ] and he met the King's family

e. Arthur and Guinevere
- [ ] sat together at the banquet
- [ ] became good friends
- [ ] were married

f. The Round Table was a gift
- [ ] from King Uther
- [ ] from King Leodegrance
- [ ] from the Saxons

g. The enormous Round Table
- [ ] had belonged to King Uther
- [ ] had places for 100 knights
- [ ] had a magic power

h. Arthur called the bravest knights of Britain
- [ ] to build his new castle
- [ ] to sit at the Round Table
- [ ] to fight against the Saxons

2 Object Pronouns （賓語人稱代詞）

Look at these sentences from Chapter 5:

He invited *him* and his knights to a royal banquet.
him refers to Arthur
Arthur fell in love with *her*.
her refers to Guinevere

There are two types of pronouns （代詞）**, Subject Pronouns** （主語人稱代詞） **(I-you-he-she-it-we-they) and Object Pronouns (me-you-him-her-it-us-them). We use object pronouns as the direct or indirect object of a verb** （動詞的直接或間接賓語） **. Choose the correct object pronouns and write them above the words in italics.**

a. Britain was in danger. A lot of enemies wanted to invade ~~Britain~~. *it*

b. Arthur helped King Leodegrance. King Leodegrance was thankful to *Arthur*.

c. King Leodegrance had a beautiful daughter. Arthur met *Princess Guinevere* at the banquet.

d. Merlin wasn't happy with Arthur's choice, but he accepted *his King's decision*.

e. King Leodegrance said, 'Thank you for protecting *me and my people.*'

f. The Round Table had places for 150 knights. Arthur called *the knights* to sit at the Round Table.

3 **Have fun with this crossword puzzle!**

Across

1. name of King Arthur's sword
2. wise magician
3. big group of soldiers
4. the Round ....

Down

5. King Arthur lived here
6. name of King Arthur's real father
7. enemies who tried to invade Britain
8. a big party where everyone eats

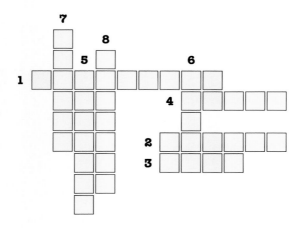

4 **Listen to the first four paragraphs of Chapter 5 and fill in the missing words.**

A lot of .... tried to invade Britain: the Saxons, the Jutes, the Pitts and others.

A big .... of Saxons attacked King Leodegrance in his castle. He was the King of Cameliard. .... King Arthur and his knights fought against these Saxons and ....

King Leodegrance was very thankful to Arthur. He .... him and his knights to a royal banquet. At the ...., Arthur met the King's daughter, Princess Guinevere. Guinevere was young and very .... Arthur fell in .... with her. He wanted to marry her.

Merlin .... happy with Arthur's choice, but he accepted his king's ....

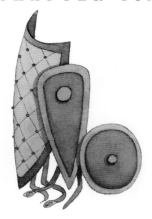

CHAPTER SIX

The five Kings

King Arthur and Queen Guinevere were very happy together. The people loved their beautiful queen.

Not long after their marriage, there was another invasion[1] of Britain. The King of Ireland, the King of Denmark, and three other kings joined together. They wanted to conquer[2] Britain with their strong armies.

'We must fight these five kings,' said King Arthur. 'We must protect Britain.'

The knights of the Round Table were ready to fight against the enemy.

Before leaving Camelot, Arthur said to Guinevere, 'Dear Guinevere, I don't want to leave you alone. Please come with me. I promise to protect you. Your lovely presence[3] gives me happiness and courage.'

---

1. **invasion**：侵略。
2. **conquer**：征服。
3. **presence**：儀態。

King Arthur
and his Knights

Guinevere smiled and said, 'Arthur, I am happy to follow you.'
Queen Guinevere rode next to King Arthur. King Arthur's
army followed. After travelling for many days
they did not meet the five kings.

Suddenly one night, the five kings attacked
King Arthur's camp [1]. They almost destroyed
the camp. The noise of the battle woke up
King Arthur. He, Guinevere, and the other
knights rode away quickly. They crossed the
River Humber and went to the forest. Then
they heard horses across the
river. In the moonlight, they saw the five
kings. The kings were riding towards
them, and they were alone.

One knight said, 'Let's attack
them by surprise [2] ! They're
alone! They can't see us, but
we can see them!'

King Arthur and his knights
killed the five kings.

The enemy armies were
confused [3] without their leaders.
They all left Britain. King
Arthur and his knights were
again victorious [4]. They saved Britain
from a dangerous [5] invasion.

---

1. **camp** : 營地。
2. **attack them by surprise** : 突襲。
3. **confused** : 混亂的。
4. **victorious** : 勝利的。
5. **dangerous** : 危險的。

UNDERSTANDING THE TEXT

1 **Decide if the following sentences are true (T) or false (F). Correct the false sentences.**

		T	F
a.	King Arthur and Queen Guinevere were happy together.	☐	☐
b.	Soon after their marriage, five kings wanted to conquer Britain.	☐	☐
c.	When King Arthur went to fight against the enemy, Guinevere stayed in Camelot.	☐	☐
d.	One night, the five kings attacked King Arthur's camp.	☐	☐
e.	Arthur, Guinevere, and the knights crossed the River Humber and returned to Camelot.	☐	☐
f.	They attacked the five kings by surprise and killed them.	☐	☐

2 **Word Puzzle**

Read the definitions and write the words.

a. very pretty, lovely: B _ _ _ _ _ F _ _

b. ruler of a country: _ _ _ G

c. opposite of weak: S _ _ _ _ G

d. take care of: P _ _ _ _ C _

e. there are many trees here: _ O _ _ S _

f. wife of a king: _ U _ _ _

g. not safe: D _ _ G _ _ _ _ S

3 Possessive Adjectives（物主形容詞）

Look at these sentences:

The people loved *their* beautiful Queen.
Not long after *their* marriage, there was another invasion of Britain.

Their **is a possessive adjective. The other possessive adjectives are:** my-your-his-her-its-our.

Fill in the gaps in the sentences below with the correct possessive adjectives.

a. Queen Guinevere rode .... brown horse.

b. 'This is .... fountain!' said Sir Pellinore.

c. 'The five kings attacked .... camp!' said the Knights.

d. Merlin wasn't happy with Arthur's choice, but he accepted .... King's decision.

e. 'Excalibur is .... new sword,' said Merlin to Arthur.

f. The noblemen did not obey .... King.

CHAPTER SEVEN

Lancelot

ne of the knights of the Round Table was Lancelot. He came from France. Lancelot was very kind and generous. He often gave his things [1] to the poor.

Lancelot served his king and queen well. One day a strange girl came to the great hall of the castle. She said to Sir Lancelot, 'Come with me! It's very important. I cannot tell you more. Please follow me.'

Sir Lancelot followed the girl to the forest. They stopped at a church.

Lancelot entered the church. He saw twelve nuns [2]. One nun said, 'Sir Lancelot, we bring you this young man. He is loyal and courageous. Please make him a knight.'

1. **things** : 財產。

2. **nuns** :

King Arthur
and his Knights

The young man looked honest. Lancelot agreed to make him

a knight. However, Lancelot did not recognize [1] this young man. He was the son Lancelot had from Elaine, a lady he loved some years before. The young man's name was Galahad. Galahad's mother wanted him to be a knight, like his father.

The next day, Lancelot returned to Camelot with the young knight. King

Arthur, Queen Guinevere and the knights of the Round Table were happy to meet Galahad.

When Sir Galahad sat down at the Round Table, his name appeared on the table! Everyone was amazed [2]. Lancelot looked at Galahad carefully. Suddenly, he realised [3] that Galahad was his son! Lancelot was very happy and proud [4].

1. **recognize**：認出。
2. **amazed**：驚訝的。
3. **realised**：認識到。
4. **proud**：自豪的。

UNDERSTANDING THE TEXT

 1 **Complete the following sentences by circling the correct words.**

a. Lancelot was a kind and *poor / generous* knight.

b. One day a *beautiful / strange* girl came to the castle.

c. She said to *Lancelot / Arthur*, 'Please *follow / help* me.'

d. Lancelot and the girl went to the *forest / lake*. They stopped at a *church / castle*.

e. In the church a *nun / man* said, 'Lancelot, we bring you this young *man / boy*. Please make him a *soldier / knight*.'

f. Lancelot agreed to make him a knight. But Lancelot did not know that it was Galahad, his *brother / son*.

g. Everyone at Camelot was *surprised / happy* to meet Galahad.

h. Suddenly, Lancelot realised that Galahad was his son. He was very *proud / confused*.

2 **A. Which adjectives**（形容詞）**or nouns**（名詞）**describe these characters? Some can be used more than once. Choose the words from the Round Table.**

Merlin	Arthur	Lancelot	Guinevere	Galahad

wife

counsellor

beautiful   wise

king   friendly

courageous   generous

magician

queen   kind

loyal   adventurous

knight

B. Now make sentences that describe these characters.

    a. Merlin is a .... He is ....

    b. Arthur is a .... He is ....

    c. Lancelot is a .... He is ....

    d. Guinevere is a .... She is ....

    e. Galahad is a .... He is ....

3   The Imperative（祈使語氣）

The Imperative in English is the same as the Infinitive of the verb（動詞原形）**, without** 'to'.
In Chapter 7, we saw these imperative sentences:

Come with me!
Please follow me!
Please make him a knight.

To form a negative imperative（否定祈使句）**, we add** 'do not', 'don't' **or** never **before the verb:**

Don't follow me!
Never go to the forest alone!

Complete the following sentences with the imperatives in the sword.

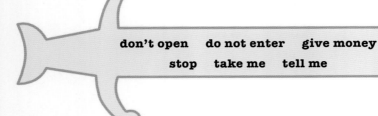

don't open   do not enter   give money

stop   take me   tell me

a. Lancelot must not enter the church. The nun says, '...................... this church!'

b. Lancelot often gave his things to the poor. He told his friends, '...................... to the poor!'

c. Galahad wanted to see King Arthur. He asked Lancelot, '...................... to him.'

d. It's very cold outside. '...................... the door.'

e. Guinevere wants to know Arthur's story. She asks him, '...................... your story.'

f. Merlin said to Sir Pellinore, '...................... fighting!'

Castles

Long ago castles were built to protect people from enemies.

The first castles were made of wood. They were small and were built on hills. There was a high fence [1] all around them.

Families lived in huts [2], in the field [3] below. When the enemy attacked, they all ran to the castle.

1. **fence** :
2. **huts** : 小屋。
3. **field** : 平地。

With time, castles were made of rocks. They were much stronger and bigger than the first castles. They had very thick walls. It was difficult for the enemy to attack this type of castle. Castles were built to protect important places. They were built on mountains and near rivers and seas.

There are many old castles in the world today. Many are open to the public [1]. It is interesting to visit old castles and see how people lived in the past.

---

1. **open to the public** ：對公眾開放。

Every castle had a dungeon [1]. It was a cold, dark place for prisoners.

Many people lived and worked in a castle. There were noblemen with their families, warriors, servants, jesters [2] and musicians. It was like a village.

1. **dungeon** : 地牢

2. **jesters** :

How much do you remember?

Across

1. members of the nobility
2. soldiers who attacked the castle
3. cold, dark place
4. people who made music in the castle
5. where ordinary people lived

Down

6. flat land
7. high area where castles were built
8. person who makes people laugh
9. a barrier

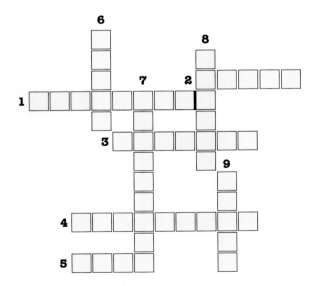

Old Castles of Great Interest

1. Bamburgh Castle was built in the 6th century in Northumberland. It was built on a high cliff[1]. It is surrounded[2] on three sides by the sea. Many films were made here.

2. Carlisle Castle was built at the end of the 11th century by William Rufus. It is near Scotland. At first, it was a wooden castle. In 1122, Henry I built walls of stone.

1. **cliff** : 懸崖。　　　　2. **surrounded** : 被包圍。

3. Dover Castle was originally [1] a fort [2], built by the Celts. Then the Romans built a lighthouse [3], which you can still visit. Later, Bishop Odo of Bayeus built the great Dover Castle.

4. Edinburgh Castle was built in Edinburgh, Scotland. In the 7th century, King Edwin built a fortress [4] on a big rock. Later, it became a great castle.

1. **originally**：最初。
2. **fort**：堡壘。
3. **lighthouse**：燈塔。
4. **fortress**：要塞。

1 **Put the name of each castle below its description.**

a. The Romans built a lighthouse here.

....

b. It is surrounded by the sea on three sides.

....

c. King Edwin built it in the 7th century in Scotland.

....

d. It was a wooden castle at first.

....

Which of these four castles do you like best? Why?

Edinburgh Castle

Bamburgh Castle

CarlisleCastle

Dover Castle

◆2 Questions for you

a. Do you like castles?

b. Why or why not?

c. Are there many castles in your country?

d. Can you name them?

e. Do you think ghosts live in some castles?

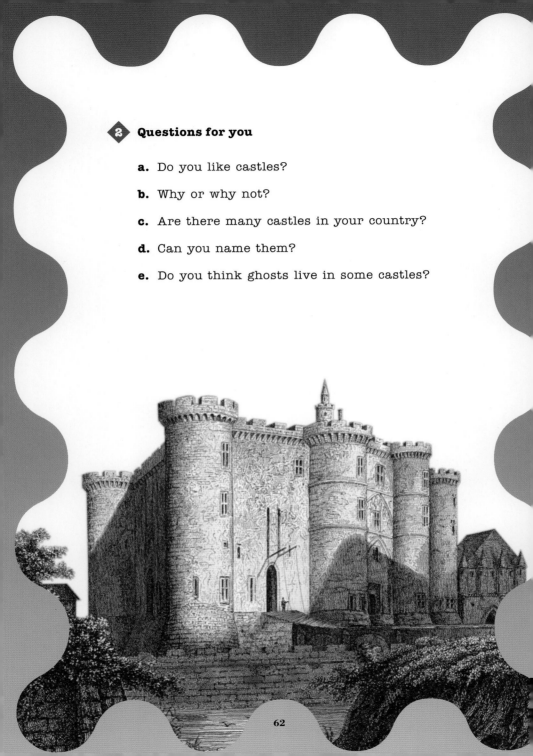

CHAPTER EIGHT

The Holy Grail[1]

ne day the knights were sitting at the Round Table. They were celebrating a religious holiday. Suddenly, there was a loud noise. Then there was a strong light.

A green bowl covered with a cloth moved around the room. Invisible[2] hands carried it. After a few moments, the green bowl disappeared[3].

'That was the Holy Grail!' exclaimed King Arthur. 'That is where Christ's blood was kept after he was crucified[4].'

The knights were amazed. They all wanted to see the Holy Grail.

Sir Gawain, a loyal knight, declared[5], 'I want to look for the

---

1. **the Holy Grail**：(傳說耶穌在最後的晚餐中用的) 聖杯。
2. **invisible**：看不見的。
3. **disappeared**：消失。
4. **was crucified**：被釘在十字架上。
5. **declared**：宣佈。

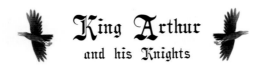
Grail for one year and one day.'

'Yes, I want to look for the Grail too,' said another knight.

All the knights wanted to travel to distant lands to find the Holy Grail. There was great excitement [1] at the Round Table.

King Arthur was very worried. He knew that the search [2] for the Holy Grail was dangerous. In fact, many knights died during the search. Others never returned to Camelot.

Only three knights found the Holy Grail. They were Galahad, Percival and Bors. All three had pure hearts. Only those with pure hearts saw the Holy Grail. The three knights travelled to distant lands. After many dangerous adventures, they found the Holy Grail.

When they saw it on a silver table, they thanked God for this great happiness. After finding the Grail, Galahad and Percival died. But Bors returned to Camelot. He told everyone about his wonderful experience.

1. **excitement**：興奮。
2. **search**：尋找。

UNDERSTANDING THE TEXT

1 **Choose the correct answer.**

a. The knights were all sitting at the Round Table. They were celebrating
☐ Christmas
☐ a religious holiday
☐ a victory

b. A green bowl covered with a cloth
☐ was on the table
☐ was on the floor
☐ moved around the room

c. King Arthur exclaimed:
☐ 'That was Christ's blood!'
☐ 'That was the Holy Grail!'
☐ 'That was the Grail from God!'

d. All the knights wanted to
☐ look for the Holy Grail
☐ travel to distant lands
☐ bring the Holy Grail to Camelot

e. The search for the Holy Grail was
☐ difficult
☐ exciting
☐ dangerous

f. The three knights who found the Holy Grail were
☐ Galahad, Percival and Bors
☐ Bors, Galahad and Lancelot
☐ Percival, Galahad and Pellinore

2 Crack the Code!

Can you discover what these words are?
Use the secret code, unscramble them, and you will find a question.

A = ♥   O = ♠
E = ☼   U = ✿
I = ★

1. ☼ r h ☼ w = _ _ _ _ _
2. s ★ = _ _
3. H ☼ t = _ _ _
4. y ♠ h l = _ _ _ _
5. l ♥ r ★ g = _ _ _ _ _
6. ♠ w n = _ _ _ ?

Do you know the answer?

3 Past Simple Passive (被動語態的過去時)

We use an active verb (主動動詞) to say what the subject does:
The Romans built the castle.
We use a passive verb (被動動詞) to say what happens to the subject:
The castle was built by the Romans.
The castle was built in 1492.
Change the following sentences into the Past Simple Passive form.

a. Invisible hands carried the Holy Grail.
The Holy Grail .... by ....

b. Only three knights found the Holy Grail.
The Holy Grail ....

c. King Edwin built the fortress.

....

d. The enemies invaded Britain.

Britain ....

e. The five kings attacked King Arthur's camp.

....

f. The knight defended the king.

....

4 **Listen to the first six paragraphs of Chapter 8 and circle the words you hear.**

One day the knights were *seated / sitting* at the Round Table. They were celebrating a religious *holiday / day*. Suddenly, there was a loud noise. Then there was a *big / strong* light.

A green *ball / bowl* covered with a cloth moved around the room. Invisible hands carried it. After a few *minutes / moments*, the green bowl disappeared.

'That was the *old / Holy* Grail!' exclaimed King Arthur. 'That is *were / where* Christ's blood was kept after he was crucified.'

The knights were amazed. They all *went / wanted* to see the Holy Grail.

Sir Gawain, a loyal knight, declared, 'I want to look for the Grail for one *month / year* and one day.'

'Yes, I want to look *for / at* the Grail too,' said another knight.

CHAPTER NINE

King Arthur goes to Avalon

ing Arthur lived a long life, but it finished sadly. In the search for the Holy Grail, many of his knights left Britain. Other knights died. Arthur was alone.

In 537, King Arthur went to a distant land to fight. Sir Gawain and other loyal knights went with him. Before leaving Camelot, King Arthur spoke to a knight called Mordred. He said, 'Mordred, I ask you to rule ¹ my land until I return. I know you are a loyal man.'

King Arthur and his knights left Britain to go to war. But

---

1. **rule**：統治。

King Arthur goes to Avalon

Mordred was not loyal. He wanted to take King Arthur's place. He wanted to be King of Britain!

So Mordred told everyone that Arthur was killed in the war, in France. Mordred became King of Britain! He was made King in Canterbury.

When King Arthur heard the news, he was furious. He returned to Britain immediately. He and his knights arrived in Dover. Here he found Mordred and his army. They were waiting for him.

There was a long, terrible battle. Only King Arthur and Sir Bedivere remained alive [1]. Sir Gawain died in Arthur's arms. The King buried [2] him in Dover Castle.

Arthur fought a long battle against Mordred.

At the end of the battle, King Arthur took his spear [3] and killed Mordred. But Mordred's sword went through Arthur's helmet [4] and his head.

The great king was dying! He still had to do one thing. He called Sir Bedivere and said, 'I must give my sword

1. **alive** : 活着的。
2. **buried** : 埋葬。
3. **spear** : 矛。
4. **helmet** : 頭盔。

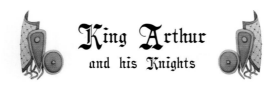

Excalibur back to the Lady of the Lake. Take it to the lake. Then throw it far into the water.'

Sir Bedivere went to the lake. He threw Excalibur far into the water. An arm came out of the water and caught the sword. Then it disappeared into the water.

Sir Bedivere returned to King Arthur. He told him about what he saw at the lake. Arthur was satisfied and said, 'Thank you, my loyal friend. Now carry me to the lake.'

At the lake, there was a boat waiting for Arthur. The Lady of the Lake was in it.

'Put me in the boat,' said Arthur. Sir Bedivere obeyed and said, 'What can I do without you, my king?'

Arthur answered, 'My life is near the end. Pray [1] for yourself! Prayers can do many things. Farewell [2]! I am going to Avalon [3].'

The boat moved away slowly. Sir Bedivere watched the boat on the lake until it disappeared.

1. **Pray**：祈禱。
2. **Farewell**：再見。
3. **Avalon**：（凱爾特神話中）西方樂土島。

UNDERSTANDING THE TEXT

1 **Are the following sentences true (T) or false (F)?**

	T	F
a. In the search for the Holy Grail, many of the knights left Britain.	☐	☐
b. In 537, Arthur went to a distant land to live.	☐	☐
c. Before leaving Camelot, King Arthur said to Mordred, 'Please rule my land until my return.'	☐	☐
d. Mordred wanted to take King Arthur's place.	☐	☐
e. Mordred told everyone that King Arthur was killed in France.	☐	☐
f. Mordred became King of Britain.	☐	☐
g. When King Arthur heard this, he remained in France.	☐	☐
h. King Arthur fought against Mordred.	☐	☐
i. At the end of the battle, Mordred died and Arthur was wounded.	☐	☐
j. Sir Bedivere hid Excalibur in the forest.	☐	☐
k. Sir Bedivere carried dying Arthur to the lake.	☐	☐
l. Arthur said, 'I am going to Camelot.'	☐	☐

2 **Fill in the blank spaces with the correct verb tense. The infinitives** (動詞原形) **are in the helmet.**

find   tell
fight   catch
hear   throw   be
bury   leave

a. Many knights .... Britain.

b. Mordred .... everyone that Arthur ....
killed in the war.

c. When Arthur .... the news, he was furious.

d. At Dover, King Arthur .... Mordred and his army.

e. The king .... Sir Gawain in Dover Castle.

f. Arthur .... a long battle against Mordred.

g. Bedivere .... Excalibur into the lake.

h. An arm .... the sword.

A medieval picture showing the deaths
of Arthur and Mordred.

3 The Contracted Form（縮寫形式）or Genitive 's（所有格）?

Sometimes we confuse the genitive 's' with the contracted form of the verbs is or has. Look at these examples:

Sir Gawain died in Arthur*'s* arms.

Here the *'s* means the *arms of Arthur.*

Arthur*'s* going to fight Sir Pellinore. **(Arthur is going to...)**
He*'s* got a big sword. **(He has got...)**

Here the *'s* means *is* or *has*

Change these sentences to the genitive *'s'*, or to the contracted verb form:

a. The life of Arthur was long.
....

b. King Arthur is going to France.
....

c. The army of Mordred was in Dover.
....

d. Sir Bedivere has taken Excalibur to the lake.
....

Now decide if the *'s* is the *genitive* or *is* or *has*.

e. The lady's bringing the boat.
....

f. Galahad's looking for the Holy Grail.
....

g. Lancelot's got many friends.
....

h. The knight's trip was dangerous.
....

4 **Summary of the story**

Fill in the gaps with the words from the Round Table, and you will have a summary of the book. Some words can be used twice.

Holy Grail   Galahad
Bors   Excalibur
stone   noblemen   pulls   magician
king   the year   married   Merlin
great church   sword
good   new   Arthur   true
written   Christmas Day
Round Table   return   Percival
Archbishop   died
Mordred   army   Avalon
disappeared

In .... 509, Britain had no .... Merlin, the
.................., went to the .... and said, 'We must have
a king. Tell all the .... of the kingdom to meet at the
.... in London on ....'

Outside the church there was a big .... with a
.... in it. These words were .... on the stone:
'He who .... the sword out of this stone is the
.... king of Britain.'

Young .... pulled the sword out of the stone. He was
the .... King of Britain. Arthur was a ....
king. His people loved him. One day Arthur and ....

75

went to a lake. Here Arthur received his famous sword, ...

Arthur .... Princess Guinevere. As a wedding gift, King Leodegrance gave Arthur the .... Only the best knights sat at the Round Table.

One day the .... appeared to Arthur and his knights. Then it ....

Three knights wanted to look for it. They were ...., ... and .... Galahad found it, but then he died.

In 537, Arthur went to France to fight. He asked .... to rule the land until his .... But .... wanted to take Arthur's place! When Arthur heard this, he returned to Britain. Here Arthur fought against Mordred and his .... Both Arthur and Mordred .... Finally, the Lady of the Lake took Arthur to ....

The Round Table

hat happened to King Arthur's Round Table? In the old castle in Winchester, there is an enormous round table. It is hanging[1] on the wall. In 1485, William Caxton, the first English printer[2], said that this round table was King Arthur's. The names of 24 knights are painted on the table. King Arthur's place has no name on it. Instead, his picture is painted on it. Some of the knights mentioned[3] on the table are: Sir Lancelot, Sir Galahad, Sir Pellinore, Sir Gawain, Sir Bedivere, Sir Ector and Sir Mordred.

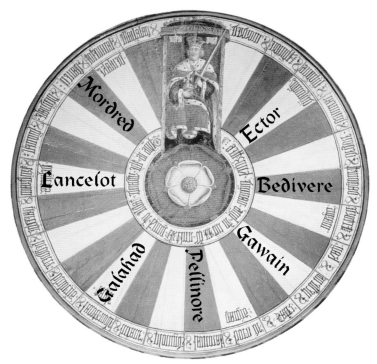

This is King Arthur's Round Table with 24 of his named Knights.

1. **hanging** : 懸掛。　　2. **printer** : 印刷商。　　3. **mentioned** : 提到。

1 **Who are they?**

Put the name(s) of the knight(s) below the description. One is done for you.

a. He fought with King Arthur near a fountain.
Pellinore ....

b. They found the Holy Grail.
....

c. He raised Arthur well.
....

d. He came from France.
....

e. He took King Arthur's place as King of Britain.
....

f. He died in Arthur's arms.
....

g. He carried dying King Arthur to the lake.
....

Where was King Arthur Buried?

At the end of the 12th century, the monks [1] of an abbey [2] in Glastonbury discovered a grave. On the tombstone [3] of this grave [4] there were these Latin words:

Hic Jacet Arthurus Rex Quondam Rexque Futurus

(Here lies Arthur, once King and King to be)

Was this King Arthur's grave? Before dying, Arthur said to

Bedivere, 'I am going to Avalon.' In a writing of the 12th century, the word Avalon meant 'the island of apples.' The name Glastonbury came from the name of a peasant, Glasteing. This peasant built a house near a big apple tree. Later, a church was built here. The name Glasteing became Glastonbury, near the River Severn. Today, Glastonbury is in the county [5] of Somerset.

The Latin words, 'Rexque Futurus' mean that King Arthur will perhaps return one day, if his people need him!

1. **monks**：修士。
2. **abbey**：修道院。
3. **tombstone**：墓碑。
4. **grave**：墳墓。
5. **county**：郡。

79

Look at the map.

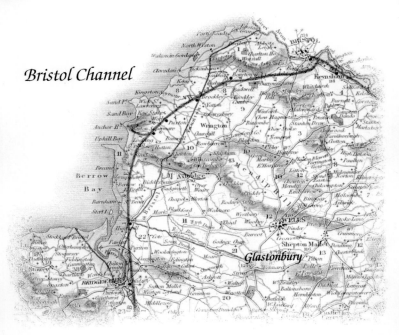

a. What is the name of the town north-east of Glastonbury?

b. What is the name of the hills north of Glastonbury?

c. If you go west from Glastonbury, where do you go?

d. Berrow Bay is part of the .... Channel.

EXIT TEST

CONTEXT

1 **Circle the correct answer.**

a. King Arthur's story is *a historical fact / a legend.*

b. The first inhabitants of Britain were the *Romans / Celts.*

c. King Arthur was a *Celtic / Roman* leader.

d. King Arthur's castle was in *Winchester / Camelot.*

e. His round table is in the *old castle / church* in Winchester.

COMPREHENSION

2 **Are the following sentences true (T) or false (F)? Correct the false sentences.**

	T	F
a. Young Arthur pulled the sword out of the stone and he became King of Britain.	☐	☐
b. Arthur didn't like adventures.	☐	☐
c. Arthur lost his sword during a fight with Sir Pellinore.	☐	☐
d. Arthur went to the lake and found Excalibur.	☐	☐
e. Princess Guinevere was King Leodegrance's sister.	☐	☐
f. King Arthur married Guinevere.	☐	☐
g. The Round Table was a gift from King Leodegrance.	☐	☐
h. Lancelot's son was Sir Galahad.	☐	☐
i. Many knights went to the Holy Land and looked for the Holy Sword.	☐	☐
j. The Lady of the Lake took the dying King to Avalon.	☐	☐

GRAMMAR

3 **Put the verbs into the Past Simple tense.**

The Knight (*be*) [1].................. an important figure in the feudal system of the Middle Ages. He (*defend*) [2].................. his king, his country and his church.

Knights usually (*come*) [3].................. from rich and noble families. They (*begin*) [4].................. their training when they (*be*) [5].................. very young as pages. They then (*become*) [6].................. squires and finally knights.

Knights (*wear*) [7].................. fine clothes and heavy armour. They (*fight*) [8].................. with a shield, a lance and a long sword. Each knight (*carry*) [9].................. a shield with a particular colour and design on it.

4 **Fill in the gaps with the following prepositions. Some words can be used more than once.**

for   near   on   in   of   around

The first castles were made [1].................. wood. They were built [2].................. hills. There was a high fence all [3].................. them. People lived [4].................. the field below, [5].................. huts. Later castles were made [6].................. big stones. Every castle had a dungeon. It was a cold, dark place [7].................. prisoners. Castles were built [8].................. rivers and seas.

WORD PUZZLE

5 Can you remember the names of five of the knights of the Round Table?
Circle their names.

F	J	L	N	C	Q	V	W	B	P	Y
P	G	A	L	A	H	A	D	S	E	C
O	M	N	A	T	H	U	T	H	L	U
A	E	C	D	B	P	S	R	K	L	G
R	I	E	C	T	O	R	Z	U	I	L
V	E	L	B	F	J	O	W	J	N	W
Z	M	O	R	D	R	E	D	G	O	E
H	S	T	H	L	O	F	Y	R	R	Z
O	X	Z	S	A	U	S	M	Q	E	U

6 Write your own sentences about King Arthur.

King Arthur was

....
....
....
....

7 What is your favourite part of the story?

....
....
....
....
....
....
....
....

KEY TO THE EXERCISES AND EXIT TEST

WAS KING ARTHUR ONLY A LEGEND?

Page 10 Exercise 1
a5 - b3 - c4 - d1 - e2.

BEFORE ARTHUR'S TIME

Page 12 Exercise 1

S	X	O	F	G	J	Z	V	R	A	O
D	S	H	A	D	R	I	A	N	G	H
B	S	R	Q	Y	P	E	D	I	H	Z
R	Z	E	J	C	A	E	S	A	R	L
I	O	X	R	L	V	R	G	Q	K	W
T	R	G	D	A	M	T	H	M	E	O
A	B	L	I	U	G	V	S	I	J	D
N	P	C	N	D	S	U	O	W	L	X
N	V	J	B	I	W	F	A	G	P	J
I	O	H	F	U	Q	P	F	B	V	C
A	U	K	I	S	E	O	P	E	R	K

BEFORE READING

Page 13 Exercise 1
Open answer.

Page 13 Exercise 2
Open answer.

CHAPTER 1
Page 17 Exercise 1

a. Uther Pendragon became King of Britain
b. King Uther's counsellor
c. Sir Ector and his wife
d. King Uther died
e. 'God will show us the new king on Christmas Day'
f. 'He who pulls the sword out of this stone is the true King of Britain'

Page 18 Exercise 2
become, have, be, die, give, raise, go, say

CHAPTER 2
Page 22 Exercise 1
a. T
b. F – Arthur was in London with Sir Ector.
c. T
d. F – All the noblemen were surprised.
e. T
f. T
g. F – Merlin said, 'This is King Uther's son and he is our new king!'

Page 22 Exercise 2
a10 - b6 - c8 - d7 - e2 - f9 - g3 - h4 - i5 - j1

Page 23 Exercise 3
a. This
b. That
c. This
d. Those

84

e. These
f. This

Page 23 Exercise 4
sword, stone, King, Britain, father, magician, knight

CHAPTER 3

Page 27 Exercise 1
a. twenty
b. Saxons, enemies
c. adventures
d. friendly, courageous
e. Pellinore
f. lances, swords
g. broke
h. Merlin, king

Page 28 Exercise 2
A.

X	K	H	E	L	D	I	C	S	J	Y	F	M
O	T	U	L	W	C	E	O	H	L	J	R	C
P	A	D	V	E	N	T	U	R	O	U	S	N
S	E	G	R	A	B	H	R	O	Y	C	P	G
G	R	P	L	O	Y	E	A	T	A	U	H	I
A	M	L	V	K	E	U	G	P	L	B	C	B
B	D	J	A	F	R	I	E	N	D	L	Y	A
S	C	K	X	O	S	K	O	V	H	R	O	S
N	Z	V	K	P	A	J	U	X	V	A	U	H
P	Q	A	J	M	I	F	S	O	Y	F	I	T
Z	I	F	B	U	N	D	B	F	M	Y	R	X

B.
a. friendly
b. courageous
c. loyal
d. adventurous

Page 29 Exercise 3
a. doesn't like eating
b. liked fighting
c. liked causing trouble
d. didn't like riding
e. likes reading
f. didn't like living

Page 29 Exercise 4

Dear Father,
Yesterday I went to the forest.
I rode my beautiful horse.
In the forest I saw a fountain.
My horse wanted to drink some water.
I met Sir Pellinore. He said 'Fight!'
I fought him but I broke my sword!
Merlin appeared and said, 'Stop fighting!'
Sir Pellinore stopped fighting immediately.
Love, Arthur

THE KNIGHT'S ARMOUR AND WEAPONS

Page 32 Exercise 1

HELMET
ARMOUR
LANCE
SHIELD
SWORD
BATTLE AXE

CHAPTER 4

Page 36 Exercise 1

a. broke, Merlin
b. lake, lake, an arm
c. the Lady of the Lake
d. took
e. greatest, magic
f. wear it, bleed

Page 36 Exercise 2

a. with
b. during
c. of, in
d. out
e. with

CHAPTER 5

Page 40 Exercise 1

a. enemies of Britain
b. King Leodegrance's castle
c. and won the battle
d. and he met Princess Guinevere
e. were married
f. from King Leodegrance
g. had belonged to King Uther
h. to sit at the Round Table

Page 41 Exercise 2

b. King Leodegrance was thankful to him.
c. Arthur met her at the banquet.
d. Merlin wasn't happy with Arthur's choice, but he accepted his decision.
e. King Leodegrance said, 'Thank you for protecting us.'
f. Arthur called them to sit at the Round Table.

Page 42 Exercise 3

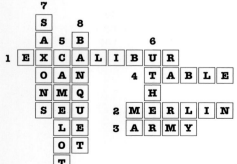

Page 43 Exercise 4

enemies, army, Young, won, invited, banquet, beautiful, love, wasn't, decision

CHAPTER 6

Page 47 Exercise 1

a. T
b. T
c. F - When King Arthur went to fight against the enemy, Guinevere followed him.
d. T
e. F - Arthur, Guinevere, and the knights crossed the River Humber and went to the forest.
f. T

Page 47 Exercise 2

a. beautiful
b. king
c. strong
d. protect
e. forest
f. queen
g. dangerous

Page 48 Exercise 3

a. her
b. my
c. our
d. his
e. your
f. their

CHAPTER 7

Page 52 Exercise 1

a. generous
b. strange
c. Lancelot, follow
d. forest, church
e. nun, man, knight
f. son
g. happy
h. proud

Page 53 Exercise 2

A.

Merlin: counsellor, wise, magician
Arthur: king, friendly, courageous, loyal, adventurous, knight
Lancelot: generous, kind, knight

Guinevere: wife, beautiful, queen
Galahad: courageous, loyal, knight

B.
a. magician / wise
b. king / courageous, adventurous, loyal and friendly
c. knight / generous and kind
d. queen / beautiful
e. knight / loyal and courageous

Page 54 Exercise 3
a. Do not enter
b. Give money
c. Take me
d. Don't open
e. Tell me
f. Stop

CASTLES

Page 58 Exercise 1

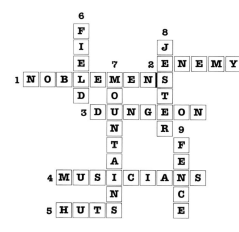

OLD CASTLES OF GREAT INTEREST

Page 61 Exercise 1
a. Dover Castle
b. Bamburgh Castle
c. Edinburgh Castle
d. Carlisle Castle

CHAPTER 8

Page 65 Exercise 1
a. a religious holiday
b. moved around the room
c. 'That was the Holy Grail!'
d. look for the Holy Grail
e. dangerous
f. Galahad, Percival and Bors

Page 66 Exercise 2
Where is the Holy Grail now?

Page 66 Exercise 3
a. The Holy Grail was carried by invisible hands.
b. The Holy Grail was found by only three knights.
c. The fortress was built by King Edwin.
d. Britain was invaded by the enemies.
e. King Arthur's camp was attacked by the five kings.
f. The king was defended by the knight.

Page 67 Exercise 4
sitting, holiday, strong, bowl, moments, Holy, where, wanted, year, for

CHAPTER 9

Page 72 Exercise 1
a. T; **b.** F; **c.** T; **d.** T; **e.** T; **f.** T; **g.** F; **h.** T; **i.** T; **j.** F; **k.** T; **l.** F.

Page 73 Exercise 2
a. left; **b.** told, was; **c.** heard; **d.** found; **e.** buried; **f.** fought; **g.** threw; **h.** caught.

Page 74 Exercise 3
a. Arthur's life was long.
b. King Arthur's going to France.
c. Mordred's army was in Dover.
d. Sir Bedivere's taken Excalibur to the Lake.
e. is
f. is
g. has
h. genitive

Page 75 Exercise 4

the year, king, magician, Archbishop, noblemen, great church, Christmas Day, stone, sword, written, pulls, true, Arthur, new, good, Merlin, Excalibur, married, Round Table, Holy Grail, disappeared, Bors, Galahad, Percival, Mordred, return, Mordred, army, died, Avalon.

THE ROUND TABLE

Page 78 Exercise 1

b. Galahad, Bors and Percival
c. Ector
d. Lancelot
e. Mordred
f. Gawain
g. Bedivere

WHERE WAS KING ARTHUR BURIED?

Page 80 Exercise 1

a. Wells
b. Mendip Hills
c. Berrow Bay
d. Bristol

1. a. a historical fact **b.** Celts **c.** Celtic **d.** Camelot **e.** Old castle

2. a. T
  b. F – He was very adventurous.
  c. F – His sword broke.
  d. T
  e. F – She was his daughter.
  f. T
  g. T
  h. T
  i. F – They went to look for the Holy Grail.
  j. T

3. 1. was **2.** defended **3.** came **4.** began **5.** were **6.** became **7.** wore **8.** fought **9.** carried

4. 1. of **2.** on **3.** around **4.** in **5.** in **6.** of **7.** for **8.** near

5.

F	J	L	N	C	Q	V	W	B	P	Y
P	G	A	L	A	H	A	D	S	E	C
O	M	N	A	T	H	U	T	H	L	U
A	E	C	D	B	P	S	R	K	L	G
R	I	E	C	T	O	R	Z	U	I	L
V	E	L	B	F	J	O	W	J	N	W
Z	M	O	R	D	R	E	D	G	O	E
H	S	T	H	L	O	F	Y	R	R	Z
O	X	Z	S	A	U	S	M	Q	E	U

6. Open answer.

7. Open answer.

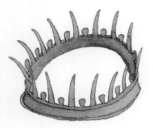

notes

notes

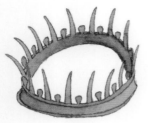 notes

 notes

This Chinese edition of *King Arthur and his Knights*
has been published with the written permission of
Black Cat Publishing.

The copyright of this Chinese edition is owned by
The Commercial Press (H.K.) Ltd.

Name of Book: King Arthur and his Knights
Told by: George Gibson
Editors: Rebecca Raynes, Elvira Poggi Repetto
Design: Nadia Maestri
Illustrations: Giovanni Manna
Edition: ©1998 Black Cat Publishing
                an imprint of Cideb Editrice, Genoa, Canterbury

系 列 名：Black Cat 優質英語階梯閱讀 · Level 2
書　 名：亞瑟王和他的圓桌武士
責任編輯：傅　伊
封面設計：張　毅
出　 版：商務印書館（香港）有限公司
　　　　　香港筲箕灣耀興道 3 號東滙廣場 8 樓
　　　　　http://www.commercialpress.com.hk
發　 行：香港聯合書刊物流有限公司
　　　　　香港新界大埔汀麗路 36 號中華商務印刷大廈 3 字樓
印　 刷：中華商務彩色印刷有限公司
　　　　　香港新界大埔汀麗路 36 號中華商務印刷大廈
版　 次：2013 年 5 月第 1 版第 6 次印刷
　　　　　© 商務印書館（香港）有限公司
　　　　　ISBN 978 962 07 1639 3
　　　　　Printed in Hong Kong

Black Cat English Readers

BLACK CAT ENGLISH CLUB

Membership Application Form

BLACK CAT ENGLISH CLUB is for those who love English reading and seek for better English to share and learn with fun together.

Benefits offered: - *Membership Card*

           - *Member badge, poster, bookmark*

           - *Book discount coupon*

           - *Black Cat English Reward Scheme*

           - *English learning e-forum*

           - *Surprise gift and more...*

Simply fill out the application form below and fax it back to 2565 1113.

Join Now! It's FREE exclusively for readers who have purchased *Black Cat English Readers* !

The book(or book set) that you have purchased: _____

English Name:_____ (Surname) _____ (Given Name)

Chinese Name: _____

Address:_____

Tel: _____ Fax: _____

Email:_____
                                  (Login password for e-forum will be sent to this email address.)

Sex: ❏ Male   ❏ Female

Education Background: ❏ Primary 1-3   ❏ Primary 4-6   ❏ Junior Secondary Education (F1-3)

                          ❏ Senior Secondary Education (F4-5)   ❏ Matriculation

                          ❏ College   ❏ University or above

Age: ❏ 6 - 9   ❏ 10 - 12   ❏ 13 - 15   ❏ 16 - 18   ❏ 19 - 24   ❏ 25 - 34

    ❏ 35 - 44   ❏ 45 - 54   ❏ 55 or above

Occupation: ❏ Student   ❏ Teacher   ❏ White Collar   ❏ Blue Collar

                 ❏ Professional   ❏ Manager   ❏ Business Owner   ❏ Housewife

                 ❏ Others (please specify: _____)

As a member, what would you like **BLACK CAT ENGLISH CLUB** to offer:

    ❏ Member gathering/ party   ❏ English class with native teacher   ❏ English competition

    ❏ Newsletter   ❏ Online sharing   ❏ Book fair

    ❏ Book discount   ❏ Others (please specify: _____)

Other suggestions to **BLACK CAT ENGLISH CLUB:**

_____

                                 Please sign here: _____

                                        (Date:_____)